SPACE TAXI

ARCHIE'S ALIEN DISGUISE

By Wendy Mass and Michael Brawer

PEACHTREE

Ⓛ Ⓑ

LITTLE, BROWN AND COMPANY
New York   Boston

Copyright © 2015 by Wendy Mass and Michael Brawer
Illustrations by Keith Frawley, based on the art of Elise Gravel

Little, Brown and Company

Hachette Book Group
1290 Avenue of the Americas, New York, NY 10104
Visit us at lb-kids.com

Little, Brown and Company is a division of Hachette Book Group, Inc.
The Little, Brown name and logo are trademarks of Hachette Book Group, Inc.

The publisher is not responsible for websites (or their content) that are not owned by the publisher.

First Edition: April 2015

Library of Congress Cataloging-in-Publication Data

Mass, Wendy, 1967– author.
Archie's alien disguise / by Wendy Mass and Michael Brawer ; interior illustrations by Keith Frawley ; based on the art of Elise Gravel. — First edition.
pages cm. — (Space taxi ; [3])
Summary: "Eight-year-old Archie Morningstar, his father, and the talking cat Pockets travel to a planet that closely resembles medieval Earth in order to rescue a princess from the clutches of the intergalactic criminal organization B.U.R.P."— Provided by publisher.
ISBN 978-0-316-24326-1 (hardback) — ISBN 978-0-316-24327-8 (ebook) —
ISBN 978-0-316-24335-3 (library edition ebook) [1. Interplanetary voyages—Fiction.
2. Adventure and adventurers—Fiction. 3. Fathers and sons—Fiction. 4. Science fiction.]
I. Brawer, Michael, author. II. Frawley, Keith, illustrator. III. Gravel, Elise, illustrator.
IV. Title.
PZ7.M42355Ar 2015
[Fic]—dc23
2014030356

10 9 8 7 6 5 4 3 2 1

RRD-C

Printed in the United States of America

For Bethany, who lovingly guides our little taxi through the cosmos.

CONTENTS

Chapter One:
Hi, My Name Is Bloppy

If you've never been woken up by your little sister lifting your eyelid with sticky peanut butter fingers, consider yourself lucky.

It's still dark, so it can't be time to wake up for school yet. Plus, it's Saturday. I try to bat Penny's hand away, but she grabs my sleeve and tugs. I groan. "Can't you see I'm sleeping?" She doesn't answer, of course. It's times like this when I wish Penny would say more than two words in a row.

"Go back to sleep, Penny."

She tugs again. I rub my eyes and look at the clock. It's 11:55 at night. I start to lie back down when it hits me.

It's 11:55 at night!

My dad and I leave in five minutes and I'm still in my pajamas! The business of ridding the universe of supervillains has been slow these days, so Dad was allowed to get back to his regular space taxi job. I am still his awesome copilot. But not if I'm late! I throw off my blanket and, by mistake, Penny with it. Oops!

"Sorry!" I say, lifting her from the floor. She just giggles. ⚡

I look around for a pair of jeans. Yesterday's clothes *should* be in a heap by my bed. Ugh, Pockets cleaned my room again. I know he is bored not saving the universe every day, but he needs to find better ways to spend his time between missions.

"Why are you even awake?" I ask Penny as I grab clothes from my drawer.

She puffs out her pink cheeks. She does this when she's about to speak. The seconds tick by. I wait as patiently as an eight-year-old who is late for a trip into outer space can wait. Seriously, I should get some kind of award. Finally she blurts, "Kitty." Then she takes a deep breath and adds, "BIG kitty."

"Yes, he is a very big kitty," I agree, pulling a sweatshirt over my head. I should have figured Pockets woke her. He insists on sleeping at the end of her bed every night. Sometimes his purring wakes up the whole family. He purrs louder than Dad snores!

I lead Penny back into her room, and she climbs into bed. "Story?" she asks.

"Sorry," I whisper. "Bedtime stories are a Mommy thing."

She curls up around her stuffed purple dragon and is asleep before I shut the door. I tiptoe to the kitchen. Mom hands me my snack and thermos, my silver space map tube, and my Intergalactic Security Force badge. "Dad and Pockets are waiting for you in the car," she says, hugging me.

"Have fun. Make good choices." The fact that Mom doesn't seem nervous anymore when I go into space makes ME a little less nervous.

"Why is Pockets with us?" I ask Dad as we head downtown in the taxi. "Aren't we just picking up a regular customer?"

"Yup," Dad says, "but Pockets couldn't miss a chance at a tuna sandwich from Barney's."

Pockets springs up from his nap. "Did someone say tuna?" He rolls down his window, takes a deep whiff, and announces, "We have arrived!"

He bounds from the car before we come to a full stop in front of the restaurant. He's already eating by the time we get inside. The man behind the counter hands Dad a slip of paper and says, "Your pickup's in the back room."

I follow Dad to a door at the end of the restaurant. It's marked KEEP OUT.

"This is where the customers who can't blend in on Earth wait for their taxis," he explains. "You can open it."

But my hands stay at my sides. What if something gigantic is waiting on the other side, ready to shoot fire out of its eyes? "It says 'keep out,'" I tell him. "And you know how Mom's always telling me not to rush into things."

He laughs. "I promise it's okay."

I take a deep breath and face the door again. An ISF deputy has to be brave, I tell myself, and slowly push open the door. All I see at first is normal stuff that you'd find in the back room of a restaurant. Shelves with napkins, pickles, and ketchup, along with a few chairs set up in front of an old TV set. I relax. "I don't think our customer is back here, Dad."

Then out of the shadows glides the blobbiest, slimiest, gooiest creature I have ever seen. Picture a melting marshmallow snowman, only orange-colored like the inside of a ripe peach. He has two large black eyes, no visible nose, and a rectangle-shaped sticker on his chest that says HI, MY NAME IS BLOPPY.

I know it's not polite to stare, but wow. I've seen some odd-looking aliens in my short time as Dad's copilot, but nothing *this* odd. A puddle of orange goo lands at his feet. I watch as more goop drips and plops to the floor.

Dad looks down at the paper in his hand, clears his throat, and says, "Hi, Bloppy, I'm Sal Morningstar. My son and I will be taking you to Libra 6 today. Looks like it will be a one-way trip?"

Bloppy begins to quiver and shake. Maybe he's getting ready to shoot fire after all! I'm not proud of it, but I sort of hide behind Dad.

But no fire comes out of Bloppy—just big, wet, goopy tears.

Chapter Two:
Change of Plans

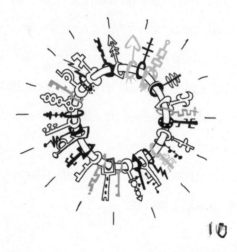

10

After about five minutes of crying and sniffling (turns out he DOES have a nose), Bloppy pulls himself together. "Sorry you had to see that," he says in a wobbly voice. "I'm starting a new job on Libra 6 tomorrow. I'm a little nervous."

"That's normal," Dad says, nodding. "I was nervous the first time I drove my taxi."

"And I was nervous the first time I had to be a copilot," I add. "I'm *still* nervous. But I love it. I bet you'll love your new job, too."

Bloppy shakes his head. "You two are lucky," he says sadly. "I know I won't like my new job selling shoes to ten-footed Orthopods, who have the smelliest feet in two galaxies, but I can't be picky. Not many choices out there for someone like me."

I guess most people don't want to hire you if you drip goop everywhere you go.

"I bet you'll feel better when we get there," Dad says. "We'll go out the back exit, and then I'll bring the taxi around."

It's a good thing Pockets has towels in

his awesome bottomless pockets. The way Bloppy is dripping, the backseat's gonna get awfully messy. But to my surprise, when we start moving to the door, all the goop on the floor slurps back up onto Bloppy's body! All that's left on the floor is a shiny glow.

That's a neat trick!

The door leads to a narrow alley, where the taxi is already waiting. Pockets jumps out of the driver's seat. Bloppy begins to quiver again.

"Cats can drive?" I ask, wide-eyed.

"Not all of them," Pockets replies. "As an ISF officer, I know how to drive more than three hundred different vehicles."

"Without the key?" Dad asks.

Pockets reaches into his fur and pulls out a huge silver circle with hundreds of keys dangling from it. "An ISF officer is always prepared."

Bloppy is now shaking all over and staring right at Pockets. Finally he shouts, "I LOVE cats!"

Before Pockets can duck, Bloppy has pulled him into a tight hug. I can barely see him—he almost completely disappears into the folds of Bloppy's blobs.

"Let me go!" Pockets shouts, but his voice is muffled, so it sounds like "Eat my toe!" Which I'm pretty sure is not what he means.

I reach over and tug on Bloppy's arm. It's less sticky than I thought it would be. "I don't think he can breathe," I tell him.

Bloppy lets go but stares adoringly. Pockets just glares. He's not the huggy type.

"Well," Dad says. "This is awkward."

"I'm sorry," Bloppy says. "On my home planet, cats are really friendly."

"Pockets is friendly," I tell Bloppy. "You just have to get to know him."

Dad opens the back door of the taxi. "Ready?" he asks.

Bloppy tries to climb in, but he's way too big to fit! Each time he squeezes one part of his body into the car, another part oozes out.

Dad and Pockets stand behind him and push. His head and belly make it in, but that's it. The rest hangs out the door. I run around to the other side of the car and grab his hands. I tug as hard as I can. My hands slide right out of his, and I fall back onto my butt.

"Are you all right, young human?" a concerned Bloppy asks from his half-in, half-out position. "Are you hurt?"

I dust myself off and reach back in. It's going to take more than *that* to keep an ISF deputy down! After another minute of pushing, pulling, and grunting, Bloppy fills every inch of the backseat. He smiles. "Whew!"

I return to my seat, exhausted, as Dad climbs into his. Pockets leans into my window. "And just where am I supposed to sit?" he asks.

I pat my knee. He sighs and climbs in. Settling on my lap, he says, "If you pet me, I'll bite."

I hold up my hands. "No petting, I promise."

Pockets sleeps through Bloppy's constant chattering about each cool thing we pass. *There are the moons of Jupiter! There goes a comet! Is that a new star?* He's fun to have along.

We're about halfway across the galaxy when the com system buzzes. "It must be Minerva calling back," Dad says. We had tried to check in with headquarters when we left, but a recorded message said Minerva was away from her desk. Dad turns the knob. "I was wondering when you'd check in, Minerva," Dad says. "We're on our way to Libra 6. Estimated time of arrival is—"

"Never mind that," a deep voice cuts him off. "You'll need to change course right away. You have a mission."

That's not Minerva's voice! I shake Pockets. "Wake up! Your dad is calling!"

Pockets jumps so high he lands on the ceiling of the car! He hangs from his claws, upside down. Bloppy and I gape at him. "That'd better not leave holes in the fabric," Dad warns.

"Father?" Pockets shouts. "Is everything all right?"

"Hello, son. I don't have time to tell you the whole story right now, so I'm beaming the information to your mini-tablet."

Pockets lands back on my lap with a thump. He reaches into a pocket and pulls out a small screen. I watch as text scrolls quickly across it.

"Morningstar!" Pockets's dad bellows.

I jump, but Dad remains calm. "Yes, Chief?" he says.

"I'm sending the coordinates straight into your navigation system. My son will fill you in on the mission. This is an emergency, so you must drop your passenger off immediately. Good luck."

A second later my map begins to shake. It's never done *that* before! I have to hold it off to the side, since Pockets is in the way. Planets and stars rise up off the page as usual, but this time a glowing red line snakes its way from our current location through two wormholes and across three more galaxies. "He wants us to go in the complete opposite direction of Libra 6!" I tell them.

"Can't be helped," Pockets says, switching off his screen. "We've got a princess to rescue."

CHAPTER THREE:
A Dark Landing

Akbar's Floating Rest Stop is only a little bit out of our way, so that's where we head to drop Bloppy off. I'm excited to see the place again. Since it's full of aliens from all over, Bloppy won't have to worry about standing out.

"You'll only be here for a few hours, tops," Dad promises Bloppy as we enter Akbar's enormous gift shop. "I left two messages at headquarters, and they'll send another space taxi to take you the rest of the way. Okay?"

Bloppy's eyes are big and round. He is actually taking the news pretty well. Personally, I think he's relieved that he's not getting to his new job so quickly.

"Do you still need this?" I ask Bloppy, pointing to his name tag.

He nods. "We all wear them where I'm from. This way we can greet everyone by name."

"I like that idea," I say, reaching over to straighten it for him. Then we all shake his hand, even Pockets. Dad presses some money into Bloppy's palm. "Go have a skate at the new rink," Dad says, pointing to a sign advertising a new roller rink at Akbar's. "Or browse the bookshop. There's always a great selection of books from across the universe."

I know Dad feels terrible about making Bloppy wait for another driver. But our jobs as ISF deputies have to come first. We wave as we back out of the gift shop. Goop splatters on the floor as Bloppy waves back. I'm sorry to leave him, too.

"This is a tricky mission," Pockets says once we're on our way. "As your map shows, we'll be going to planet Tri-Dark. This planet—like Earth—is not aware of alien life in the universe. It is like life in medieval times, with castles and knights and horse-drawn carts. We'll have to hide our modern technology and disguise ourselves."

"Awesome!" I shout. "Can I be a knight? I've always wanted to wear armor and swing a sword." *24*

He shakes his head. "You'll need more than costumes to blend in. I will alter your molecular structure with my Atomic Assembler."

"I only understood two words in that sentence," I tell him.

"I will make you look different," Pockets says plainly.

"What about you?" Dad asks him.

"They have cats on Tri-Dark, so I have no need to change."

"So you still get to be you," Dad says, "while Archie and I get turned into aliens?"

"Pretty much," Pockets admits. "But I will have to pretend to be a normal house pet again, so it won't be all fun and games for me, either." 25

"I'll promise not to scratch you behind the ears, if that helps," Dad says, grinning. "So, what's the mission?"

"King Argon owns a long walking stick— it's like a cane—that he calls the Staff of Power," Pockets begins. "He claims that it has magical powers and that it once destroyed a forest. I don't think it's true. Magic is only science that's not yet understood."

"So says the talking cat!" I comment.

Pockets pretends to ignore me and continues. "Anyway, B.U.R.P. must believe the staff has some kind of power—they took the king's only daughter, Princess Viola, and sent a ransom note insisting he hand over the staff in exchange for her safe return. We will have to find her before he gives the staff to B.U.R.P. Our undercover ISF agent was able to send the princess's last known location before his signal disappeared."

I quickly look at the map again. "A few more minutes until we cross into Tri-Dark's atmosphere. If the people there don't know about aliens and spaceships, what will happen when they see our taxi land?"

"They have not invented electric lights yet," Pockets replies. "So the planet will be totally dark at night. Can you fly this thing without the headlights?"

"Fly, yes," Dad says. "Land? No. I guess I should say I've never had to find out."

"No time like the present, then," Pockets says. "How long till we enter the atmosphere, Archie?"

"About three minutes."

"Not much time," he says. "Use your map to find a safe spot to land where our approach might be hidden."

I tap the image of the planet floating above my right knee. It gets larger. I stretch it out until I can see details like buildings and rivers. "Here!" I point to a wooded area with a clearing in the middle. "It's behind a large hill and looks far away from everything else."

"Good," Pockets says. "That hill should block us in case anyone is looking up. Now turn off the lights."

Dad and I exchange a quick glance, and

then we are in total darkness. The can't-even-see-my-hand-in-front-of-my-face kind of darkness. "Um, how am I supposed to guide us down to the surface if I can't see the map?"

"Night vision goggles!" Pockets declares, handing a pair to each of us.

"Why didn't you tell us earlier that you had these?" Dad asks.

"I can't be expected to remember *every-thing* in these pockets!" he replies.

We quickly put them on. The dark out-line of the planet rises up right in front of us! Dad tilts the wings and lowers the wheels to slow us down, but we're coming in fast. My first reaction is to shut my eyes tight from fear, but I'm pretty sure that won't help me guide the taxi. I force myself to check the map. "We're only about three hundred feet away, Dad."

I point out the window and shout, "There's the clearing!" A few seconds later, the wheels touch ground. Instead of gliding along smoothly, though, the taxi bumps up and down. It sounds like rocks are hitting the underside of the car.

When we roll to a stop, Dad shuts off the engines. No one moves.

Then Pockets asks, "Does anybody else smell popcorn?"

Chapter Four:
Is There Something Different About Me?

Apparently, if you drive over a cornfield, the heat from your car will pop some of the kernels. Woo-hoo! I open the door and take a deep breath. Nothing better than freshly popped popcorn! "Can we eat some?" I ask Dad as we all climb out. "It smells *soooo* good!"

"Not a chance," Dad says. "What would your mother say if I let either of you eat something that I drove over with the car?"

Pockets and I share a disappointed look, but I guess I can see his point.

"That's the way into town," Pockets says, pointing to a road leading away from the clearing. The goggles make everything look shades of red, but I can see almost as well as in daytime. He checks his screen. "The princess was last seen about a mile away. That's where we'll start searching in the morning. For now let's move the car as close to the woods as possible."

"Will do," Dad says, climbing back in. A few seconds later the car makes a whirring sound, followed by a chugging sound.

He tries again. Now a high-pitched whine fills the air. It sounds even squeakier than Minerva the mouse from headquarters.

Dad climbs back out. "Something must have gotten damaged when we landed," he says. He lies down on his back and slides under the car. A few minutes later he comes out, wiping grease and dirt off his face.

"I can repair it," he says, "but it will take a day or two." He turns to me. "I'll need to stay with the taxi, Archie. Do you want to go on the mission with Pockets? I know he will protect you. Or you're welcome to stay with me."

I can tell it's not easy for Dad to give me the choice to go without him. And honestly, my first reaction is to wrap myself around his leg and tell him I'll stay. But Pockets can't talk to anyone on this planet. He'll need me along to help. Plus, I want to see the knights in shining armor and the moats and the castles, and I'd miss all that if I stayed here.

"I'll go on the mission, Dad," I tell him, hoping I sound braver than I feel.

"That's the spirit, Archie!" Pockets says, slapping me on the back. "Now, let's get this car hidden before our cover is blown."

Even with Pockets's mega-strength, it takes a lot of huffing and puffing to roll the taxi across the field to the woods. When we finally get there, Pockets pulls out a skinny metal can. He shakes it and aims the nozzle into the air. A light mist sprays out and coats the entire car. Before

I can blink, the car shimmers brightly, then disappears!

"Where'd the taxi go?" I ask, eyes wide behind my goggles.

"It's still here," Pockets says. "You can touch it."

"Really?" I reach out my hand and slowly lean in. Sure enough, my hand touches the still-warm hood. "Wow! What is that stuff?"

"It's called Camo-It-Now." He tucks the can away. "It makes whatever you spray blend into the background."

I run my hand over the invisible car. This is so cool! I could do this all night!

"Come," Pockets says, as though reading my mind. "I suggest we all get some sleep. I'll wake you at dawn."

In less than a minute, Pockets has set up two inflatable mattresses with sleeping bags on them. He waits until I take off my goggles and climb into one of them, and then he curls up at the bottom.

"You are one handy cat to have around," Dad says, fluffing his pillow. But Pockets is already purring in his sleep and doesn't hear.

Dad's own snores soon join in. I stare into the night sky. Without any lights or pollution, the stars in this galaxy are so bright. I can't see the constellations I know from home. No Big Dipper or Orion's Belt. That's the last thought I have before Pockets jumps on my chest and says, "Rise and shine, young Morningstar!"

"Oomph!" I push him off. "Really, Pockets? Don't you know how much you weigh?"

Pockets jumps on Dad next. "Five more minutes," he mumbles.

"No can do!" Pockets says, sounding way too cheery for this early hour. I sit up, still groggy. The sun is just beginning to rise. It looks a lot like Earth's sun, maybe a little bigger.

"We've got to turn you into aliens," Pockets says, "then find the princess and keep the king from handing over the Staff of Power. All before breakfast!"

Dad and I climb out of our sleeping bags and stretch.

Pockets fiddles with something that looks like a television remote, but I'm pretty sure it's not. "Now stand still," he says. "This won't hurt a bit."

Before I even finish yawning, a buzzing runs through my body, followed by a not-so-gentle tugging. It's as though my arms and legs are being pulled in different directions. I try to talk, but my mouth won't move. I look to Dad for help, but Dad doesn't look like Dad anymore! I mean, I can still tell it's him, but instead of his brown hair and the goatee on his chin, he is bald with a bushy green beard. He also has three large eyes, all in a row. And is that...? Yup! A third arm has sprouted below his left one.

And did I mention he's wearing a dress?

"Archie! Is that you?" Dad blinks.

"It's me, Dad!" I wave my arms. Thankfully I have only two, but they seem longer than they used to. When I rest them at my sides, they reach my knees! 40

"Why don't I have three arms, too?" I ask.

"People here don't grow them until they're adults," Pockets explains.

Dad reaches for his face with his extra arm. He gives a little gasp when he finds the third eye between his other two. I suddenly realize I can see things to my left and right that I should only be able to see by turning my head! "Do I have three eyes, too?" I ask him.

"You sure do," Dad says. "And long orange hair." I can tell he's trying not to laugh. "Maybe you should braid it to keep it off your face," he suggests.

I swing my head from side to side. My hair reaches past my shoulders! I like to keep my hair on the longer side, but this is crazy!

"That must be how boys wear it here," Pockets says. "The Atom Assembler is programmed to keep up with the local customs."

Dad looks down at his legs. "Is that why I'm wearing this dress?"

Pockets chuckles, then shakes his head. "That's awkward. Let me fix my error."

He adjusts a knob on the assembler. Dad's legs jerk a bit, and suddenly he's wearing long brown pants, like the ones I have on.

Dad looks down, relieved. Then his hand flies up to his head. He finally realizes his hair is gone. Dad is very proud of his hair. "It'll grow back, right?" he asks Pockets in a panicky voice.

"You will return to normal at the end of our mission," Pockets promises, tucking the assembler into a pocket. "Now we really must be on our way."

Dad pulls me aside. "Listen to what Pockets tells you," he says. "And don't go off on your own. We don't know the rules here."

"Okay." This will be the first time I've been on an alien world without Dad for longer than a few minutes. He gives me a three-armed hug, which feels weird but not altogether bad.

Chapter Five:
That Is the Biggest Cat
I Have Ever Seen

We head down the road toward the village. "Remember," Pockets says, "when we get to town I'll have to pretend to be your pet. I will stay close and whisper instructions. Don't talk to anyone or attract too much attention."

"I won't," I promise.

By the time we get into town, the main square is filling with men and women setting up booths to sell food and clothes. If it weren't for all the extra eyes and arms, I'd feel as if I'd stepped back in time on Earth.

Pockets is winding in and out of my legs like a regular cat. He whispers, "The last signal we got from our undercover officer came from a farmhouse on the other side of the town square. That will be our first stop."

I nod as we begin to cross the square. No one gives us a second glance. My disguise must be working!

Two boys—both with three eyes and long hair the same green as Dad's beard—run out of a house across the lane. They begin tossing a ball between them. One misses and the ball rolls right to my feet. I pick it up. It's made of wood, and very rough. The boys run over, and I hold it out to them. It makes me miss playing baseball with my friends at home. I haven't seen them very much lately.

"That is the biggest cat I have ever seen!" the older boy says, ignoring the ball. "Much bigger than the ones at the haunted castle by the river."

Haunted castle? That doesn't sound like a fun place to hang out.

The boy bends down beside Pockets. "Might my brother and I pet him?" he asks.

"Um, okay," I say. So much for not talking to anyone!

Pockets growls, and the boy stops, his hand outstretched.

"Pockets!" I say, like I'm scolding a real pet. "Not nice."

Pockets glares up at me before lowering his head so the kids can pet him.

"So soft!" the younger boy says, stroking Pockets on the head. The older one starts scratching Pockets under the neck. After a few seconds Pockets actually starts purring!

"Why does he have a circle of green around his tail?" the younger brother asks.

"Um..." I say, trailing off. I can't tell them the truth—that laser beams shoot out of it!

"Would you like to join our game?" the older one asks.

"Really? Thanks!"

Pockets stops purring and nudges me hard in the leg. The boys start explaining the rules. Pockets is working himself into a frenzy, turning in circles and pawing at the ground.

The boys look at him, concerned. "I think something is wrong with your cat," the younger one says. "That happened to ours right before he coughed up half a mouse."

Pockets makes a coughing-choking sound, and the boys scamper backward.

"Guess I'd better go take care of him," I tell them. "Nice meeting you!"

Pockets takes off across the square, and I run after him. He doesn't slow down until we reach a big red farmhouse on the outskirts of town, right where he said the ISF guard had disappeared.

I sit down and rest against the wall of a wooden storage shed.

"We must hurry to find the undercover guard," Pockets says, looking back down at his tracking device. "Where did he go after leaving this spot?"

"I don't think he went anywhere. Come listen." I wave him over to the shed, and we press our ears against the side.

"Snoring!" Pockets exclaims. He steps back and crouches low to the ground. Then he springs into the air, arches his back, and lands on the ledge of a small window. He swishes his tail around until it's in front of him, unhinges the tip, and uses the laser beam to melt a large hole in the glass. With a satisfied glance, he squeezes in.

I, however, use the door that is about

a foot away from the window. And not locked. When I step inside, he says, "Well sure, anyone could get in *that* way."

The small shed holds only three things— a bale of hay, a broken wheelbarrow, and the sleeping ISF officer with his back against the far wall.

"He's a cat!" I say in surprise. He looks like a bigger, grizzlier Pockets. He's definitely seen some action.

"Why are you surprised?" Pockets asks.

"You said there are ISF branches in every galaxy, so I figured he would be a different kind of alien."

"That makes sense," Pockets says. "But the best of the best are from Friskopolus." He says this last part with obvious pride. He bends down beside the giant cat. "This is Hector. He was in training with my dad. Good officer. A little grumpy."

"But if he was undercover as an alien, why is he back in his cat form?" I ask.

Pockets looks around and points to a yellow-tipped dart lying next to Hector. "Aha! Sleep serum! It reversed the Atom Assembler's changes. Perhaps he left us a clue before the serum took hold."

He whips out two of his huge magnifying glasses and says, "Look for anything unusual."

"Like this?" I ask, holding my magnifying glass over a patch of dust next to Hector's left paw. Spelled out in the dirt are the words GHOST CASTLE.

"That must be the same place the boys were talking about!"

"What better place to hide than where everyone is afraid to go?" Pockets says. "Excellent work, ISF deputy Morningstar!"

"Aw, I just got lucky," I say. "I saw his paw was stretched out, so I followed it, and there were the letters."

"That's not luck," Pockets says. "You recognized a clue, and it led to a bigger clue. That's what a good detective does." He pulls out a blanket and lays it over Hector. Then he tucks a small green teddy bear under the giant cat's arm. "That'll give him a chuckle when he wakes up," Pockets says before hurrying out the door.

Chapter Six:
I Didn't Know Princesses Did That!

54

The river is about three miles away, and after mile two I'm hungry and, honestly, a little cranky. I'm tired of pushing the long hair away from my face, where it's started to stick from sweat. I've already snapped at Pockets twice just for pointing out the local plants and flowers. Finally he says, "Here, take this," and pulls out a paper bag. It's my snack from Mom! I thought I'd left it in the car.

"You're the best, Pockets." I hungrily chow down on Mom's famous peanut butter pancakes and slurp the hot chocolate. Much better! We finally reach the castle grounds and are greeted with painted wooden signs.

STAY AWAY.
TURN AROUND NOW.
DON'T EVEN THINK OF GETTING
ANY CLOSER.

The castle walls are a tall, thick gray stone covered in green moss and ivy. The surrounding garden is full of dead plants and withered vines. It is not a welcoming place.

Pockets motions for me to join him behind a large tree. From here we can spy on the castle without being seen. Spying is actually a lot less exciting than I thought it would be. Basically, we stare at the old building and wait. I whisper to Pockets, "What's the point of having three eyes if they don't do anything cool like see through walls?"

"Good idea," he replies. He pulls out a pair of X-ray glasses and peeks around the side of the tree. If you've never seen a cat wearing X-ray glasses, it is truly something to behold.

"These aren't working," he says, stashing the glasses away. "That can only mean the

X-rays are being blocked. No one from Tri-Dark would be able to do that. B.U.R.P. must be inside."

I gulp. Something black darts past us, so close it stirs a little breeze on my legs. "What was that?" I ask, jumping to my feet.

Suddenly, more shapes come out of the woods. We are surrounded! But not by ghosts or knights or evil B.U.R.P. members.

We are surrounded by cats! Regular, normal-size cats who don't talk and don't carry a carload of stuff inside their fur.

They stream past us toward the castle. Pockets and I exchange a look, then run after them, careful to stay hidden by the trees. We find the cats pacing and meowing in front of a large wooden door.

"Someone must be feeding them," Pockets whispers.

Cat-loving criminals? That's a new one.

Sure enough, a minute later the door creaks open, scraping against the stone floor. An arm shoots out, leaves a bowl of milk, and shoots back inside. It reappears and adds another bowl, this one filled with brown lumps of meat. The cats crowd around, eagerly eating and drinking. The door opens a little further, and a small figure dressed in a black cape steps halfway out and looks around. Pockets and I scoot behind the tree again.

"Good kitties," a boy's voice says softly. "Aren't you such good kitties? Yes you are, yes you are!"

We risk another look. A hood covers

most of the boy's face, but from what I can tell, he doesn't seem to have long bright-colored hair. I can't see if he has three eyes or not. He takes turns to pet each of the cats, even the ones that have scraggly, tangled fur. 60

"This is our chance," Pockets whispers. "I'll blend in with the cats, then slip inside while the door's still open. When it is safe, I will unlock the door and let you in."

I look from Pockets to the group of cats and back again. "You don't look anything like those cats. You may not realize this, but you look—how should I put this?—very well fed."

He sucks in his cheeks. "How 'bout now?"

I laugh. "Nope. You're still huge."

"Maybe he won't notice," Pockets says. He lowers himself as far as he can get to the ground without lying down, then slinks toward the castle. Now he looks like a cat pretending to be a snake. Yeah, I'm pretty sure the kid's gonna notice him.

The cloaked boy's back is turned, and for a few seconds Pockets actually does manage to mingle. A few cats sniff the new arrival, but most are too busy eating to notice. A little black cat catches sight of Pockets and starts meowing. Pockets tries to gently bat his admirer away, but he keeps coming back, rubbing up against Pockets's legs and looking up adoringly. The boy turns to see what is causing the commotion.

"And who are you?" he asks, bending to

scratch Pockets on his head. "I haven't seen you around here, and you are not easy to miss! You're very soft. Are you someone's lost pet?"

Pockets meows in response, then squeezes between the boy's legs and pretends to head toward the bowl of milk. The boy turns away, and Pockets darts through the door. The little black cat trots right in after him. A moment later the dishes are empty and the boy returns inside. The cats slowly scatter.

I run from behind my tree and try the door.

Locked.

I lean against the rough stone wall and push the hair away from my face for the hundredth time. Maybe I *should* have let

Dad braid it! Who knows how long it will take Pockets to get me in? Maybe this is one of his tests where he makes me see if I can figure it out by myself. If it is, I don't want to fail. I look around again. I really am alone here.

There's a window about twenty feet above me. I'm going to have to climb the walls by digging my fingers and toes into the little cracks between the stones. I bet my extra-long arms will help make it easier. I take a deep breath, pretend I'm a brave knight on a quest, and slip off my shoes before I can chicken out.

GASP!

I only have two toes! And they're really far apart, like one is where the big toe would go and one is where the pinkie would go. Only these both look like big toes. I flex them and they move, like they've always been there. *So weird!*

Before I have a chance to test how well they would grip the wall, something lands on my head. It's a rope!

I look up to find Pockets sticking his head out the window. He waves for me to take the rope. I'm slightly disappointed that I won't get to try scaling the wall, but only slightly.

I quickly slip my shoes back on and begin to climb the rough rope. I tell myself this is not at all like the time in gym class when I tried to climb the rope and my shorts fell down in front of the whole class. "Nope," I say out loud, "not like that at all." I soon reach the top and am proud to say that my pants are still safely around my waist.

The room is cramped and dark. The walls are covered with paintings and tapestries showing scenes of knights having jousts.

"Seen any ghosts yet?" I ask, landing on the carpeted floor with both feet.

Pockets shakes his head. "But I did find the princess. She's being kept in a room upstairs."

"And you made a friend!" I say, pointing to the little black cat who had followed Pockets into the castle.

"Very funny," Pockets says. "He won't leave me alone."

I bend down to pet the cat, but he pulls back and rubs up against Pockets instead.

"Now listen," Pockets says. "We have to find a way to get to Princess Viola. There are two B.U.R.P. guards standing outside her room. We should—"

But before he can finish talking, the door creaks open and my heart starts thudding. Pockets pushes me into a dark corner of the room. I hold my breath.

"There you are, big kitty!" the boy's voice says. To my horror, he swoops Pockets into his arms, groaning a little at the cat's weight, and carries him out of the room! The door swings shut behind them, but not before I hear the boy say, "We're going to play together all day!"

For a minute I don't move. The little black cat is pawing at the closed door, meowing. Do I go after them? What would

Pockets want me to do? I replay the scene in my mind. Pockets could have defended himself. He could have used any of the gadgets in his pockets, or even his own strength to fight off the boy, but he didn't. He just pretended to be a regular cat. That must mean he had something to gain by being taken. The only thing I can think of is that by going along, he'll be able to find out what B.U.R.P. plans to do with the Staff of Power once they get it.

That means that it's up to *me* to rescue the princess!

I think for a minute, looking around the small room. I don't see any way out besides the window and the door. I wish I'd thought to bring my space map. It worked when we were flying underwater on the planet

Nautilus; maybe it would have shown me how to get to the princess.

It's doubly hard to think because the little black cat is running in circles around the room and it's making me dizzy. He finally darts over to one wall and starts pawing at a tapestry hanging there. If he keeps pulling on it, he's going to rip the fabric. He finally nudges it aside and ducks behind it. I look closer. Where'd he go?

I pull the tapestry back, and instead of seeing the wall behind it, I spot an open doorway! Pockets's new friend found a secret passageway! He must have felt a breeze. I'll have to remember that for the next time I find myself locked in a maybe-haunted castle. I pause for only one more second, then run straight through, letting the tapestry fall into place behind me.

This turns out to be a mistake. It's completely dark in here. If only I'd thought to bring those night vision goggles!

After a minute my eyes begin to adjust. I blink. Yes! I can see the outline of the damp stone walls and the uneven steps in front of me. I rub my eyes, and things get even clearer. These new eyes may not be able to see through walls, but they can see in the dark!

I scramble up the stairs, not knowing where I'm headed, just that I have to go up. The stairwell twists and turns. I find the black cat curled up on a stair, cleaning his ears with his paw. He doesn't even glance up as I step past him.

I stop when I hear a faint noise coming from the other side of the wall. It sounds like...burping? Do ghosts burp?

There it is again, followed by a brief giggle.

"Ack!" I jump back as something soft rubs against my leg. It takes a second to realize it's only that cat again! But now I can't keep my balance, and I go headfirst into the wall beside me.

Only it *isn't* a wall! It's a door painted to *look* like a wall! The door swings open, and I go crashing right through it.

I land hard on the stone floor of a brightly lit room. A yellow-haired, three-eyed girl stands above me with her hands on her hips. She glares at me, burps, and says, "Ever heard of knocking?"

Then she burps again.

This princess is *nothing* like the ones in the fairy tales!

Chapter Seven:
The Great Escape

I quickly jump to my feet. "Sorry to burst in," I say, rubbing my sore butt. Then I stop, because that looks weird. "But hey, I found you!"

She looks me up and down as the little black cat winds in and out of her legs. Her face softens. "Yes, you found me. But who ARE you? I've never seen you before. You're not with *them*, are you?" On the word *them*, she crumples her nose like she smells something bad.

"No, no, I'm here to rescue you," I promise her.

She glances down at her boots. "And this is your cat?"

I shake my head. "I'm actually here with a different cat. He has bottomless pockets."

"Huh?" she asks.

Why did I say that? "Never mind," I add quickly. "Let's just get out of here before they find us."

"Sorry about the burping before," she says, grabbing her cloak from the back of a chair. "You wouldn't believe the gassy stuff they've been feeding me! Beans and broccoli for every meal!"

"It's all right," I say. "I have a three-year-old sister. You wouldn't believe the things that come out of her."

She smiles and says, "I can't believe I didn't think to check for any secret doors in the walls. I feel foolish."

"Don't feel bad. B.U.R.P. is very tricky."

"We're still talking about my burping?" she says. "I said I was sorry. I know it's not very princess-like."

"No, no, this is a different kind of burp. It's the name of the group who took you."

The princess's brows squish together in confusion. "No one *took* me. I was invited here by circus performers," she says. "They were dressed up in colorful costumes and masks, and they invited me to come see a play they were performing at the haunted castle." She pauses, then grumbles, "Never did see any play."

I tilt my head toward her. "Didn't your parents ever tell you not to go wandering off with strangers?"

"Yes, smarty-pants. But my bodyguard said it was okay."

I think of Hector asleep in that shed. Somehow I don't picture him letting her go off with anyone. "Did he really?"

She looks down. "Well, no. But he wasn't around for some reason and I wanted an adventure. I admit, it didn't turn out so well. Why would they keep me here?"

"Basically, they're after the Staff of Power," I tell her. "But we really need to leave now."

Her eyes widen. "What would a group of circus performers want with the Staff of Power?"

I roll my eyes. This girl is *not* getting it. "They aren't circus performers," I explain as patiently as possible. "B.U.R.P. is a criminal organization trying to take over the universe."

"What's a universe?"

Oops! I can't explain what the universe is without telling her about all the other planets and galaxies, and I'm sure that Pockets would forbid that. So I just shake my head and say, "I'll explain later. We have to go."

She nods and runs down the stairs ahead of me. Her heavy boots clatter loudly on the stairs, and I want to suggest maybe she take them off, but I'm not going to tell a princess what to do.

We haven't gotten very far when we hear, "Stop right there!" We double our speed. I have no idea where the stairs actually lead. Hopefully not to a solid stone wall. Or a dungeon!

Suddenly, laser beams go shooting over our heads! The princess blinks in shock and stumbles on the stairs. "What is that? I've never seen a light so bright."

I reach out to steady her. "Um, maybe the sun is shining in through cracks in the walls?" I hold my breath, hoping she buys that story.

"I guess," she says uncertainly.

"The staff is ours," a man's voice shouts. "There's no escape!"

"I recognize that voice," the princess says. "He's one of the circus performers!"

This time I don't bother to correct her. Especially since the man might be right! I don't see any escape.

"Oh yes there is!" another voice shouts from below. *This* voice I know! Pockets bursts into view, waving us forward. As soon as we pass by him on the stairs, he pulls out a gadget I've seen him use once before—the invisible force field! He aims it at the stairs above us. One after the other, the two men who were chasing us run right into it! They bounce backward and wind up tangled together, shouting and waving their arms and legs. The princess looks at Pockets, and then at the men who *don't* have three eyes who just ran into something she can't see. Then she crumples gracefully to the floor.

"Quick," Pockets shouts. "Grab her and follow me."

"But she's as big as me," I say, bending down. "What if I drop her?"

"You're stronger than you look," he says.

He's right! My arms aren't only long, they're really strong! I easily lift the princess and carry her over my shoulder. The B.U.R.P. guys are still trapped behind the force field, but it won't take long till they figure out a way around it.

I hurry after Pockets, who has found a

back door. Once outside he heads right for the stables and unties a huge white horse from a post. A rickety-looking wooden cart is attached to the horse with a frayed rope.

Pockets points to the cart. "Are you okay riding back there with the princess?"

I'm really not. It looks like a carnival ride my mother would never let me go on. "Do I have a choice?" I ask.

"Certainly," he says, slipping his paws in the spurs. "You can always stay here with B.U.R.P., the ghosts, and a lot of hungry cats."

Suddenly, the cart doesn't look so bad. Holding the princess, I climb in. It sags and groans under our weight.

The horse starts to move. We don't even get off the castle grounds before the

back door bangs open. "Hurry," I shout to Pockets. "They got around the force field!"

The princess stirs. Her eyes flutter open. She takes in the scene around her, and then her eyes bulge. "Is that a giant cat riding horseback?" she asks.

I nod.

"And the men with the strange lights are chasing us?" she asks, looking out the back of the cart as it bounces down the dirt road.

"Yes," I say. "And there's a boy our age here, too, somewhere."

The men are getting closer. I can see their faces clearly now. They look close to human, but with longer noses and shorter legs.

"But...but what happened to them?"

she asks with a shaky voice. "Where's their middle eye? And why do they only have two arms?"

I try to think fast. "Um, maybe they come from far away where people look different? You know, like from the other side of the river."

She shakes her head. "I've been to the other side of the river. My bodyguard, Hector, takes me there sometimes for jousting lessons. Girls aren't supposed to joust, but Hector's the best. So I know they don't have two-armed, two-eyed men and cats who ride horseback there."

The men start firing their lasers again. One beam burns a hole in the side of the cart! The princess and I scramble away from the flames. Pockets whirls around and with one paw shoots a stream of foam to put out the fire.

The princess begins breathing heavily, her eyes wild with surprise. The men can't keep up with our horse and finally fall behind.

"I'm going to take a shortcut to the castle," Pockets shouts to us. "It'll be a bumpy ride, but we must get there before B.U.R.P. does, and we don't want to be seen!"

The princess turns to ask me, "Did that cat just talk to us? I thought I heard him speak on the stairs, but I figured I imagined it."

I nod, since obviously I can't deny it. "Yeah, he can do that. I know, it's weird."

"Really weird," she agrees.

"His name is Pockets," I tell her.

She smiles. "Let me guess—he's the cat with the bottomless pockets?"

I know she's teasing me, but I don't mind. "Yup," I say.

"So I know your cat's name, but I don't know *your* name," she says. "Are you training with my father to be a knight?"

I laugh. "No. I mean, I wish I were. I'm just a regular kid. My name is Archie Morningstar."

Pockets suddenly cuts to the left, across the nearest farm. He wasn't kidding about it being bumpy. The princess and I bounce nearly three feet in the air.

"Sorry about that," Pockets shouts back at us.

"Well," the princess says, gripping the

sides of the cart tightly, "I did want an adventure!"

I can't believe it, but we make it to the princess's castle without losing a wheel or throwing up or being attacked by B.U.R.P. again. The king and a dozen knights in armor come streaming out of the front gate. This castle is about *ten times* the size of the haunted castle. It's the biggest building I've ever seen up close.

The king is wearing a tall gold crown and a red cape. The Staff of Power must be the thin metal pole he is waving above his head. I expected it to be covered in gold and jewels, but it doesn't look much different from the rod that holds up the curtains in our living room.

Before she jumps out of the cart,

Princess Viola leans over and whispers, "I'm pretty sure you're not just a regular kid, Archie Morningstar. Thank you for rescuing me." And then she kisses me on the cheek!

My hand flies up to my face, and I'm sure that my cheeks must be bright red. Pockets chuckles from atop his horse.

The princess runs up to her father and they hug. Then the king turns to us. "I demand to know what is going on. First my daughter stays out all night, worrying me to no end, and now what looks like a giant cat returns her on my missing guard's horse."

"The cat can talk!" the princess tells her father. "I've heard him!"

"Meow?" Pockets says meekly.

The princess puts her hands on her hips and glares at Pockets. "Very funny. I heard you before."

"She's telling the truth," a deep voice says from behind us. I whirl around to find Hector, the ISF bodyguard. And he's holding up the two B.U.R.P. guys by their shirt collars, one in each paw. The boy in the black cape must have escaped. "Are you all right, Princess Viola?" Hector asks.

The knights draw their swords and form a protective circle around the king and the princess. The princess stares at the huge cat from inside the circle of knights. "Hector?" she asks. "Is that you? It sounds like you, but how can it be that you are a cat now, when before you were a man?"

"It is still me, Your Highness," Hector says, bowing slightly. "I am sorry to have hidden my true identity from you, but it was for the betterment of your world. I am an Intergalactic Security Force officer. I was sent here to protect you and the Staff of Power." He tilts his head at Pockets. "The talking cat you mentioned is a fellow ISF officer. He was sent here to help."

In one swift move, Pockets leaps off the horse and onto the back of one of the bad guys. A second later, the guy is in handcuffs. Hector does the same with the other guy.

The king looks from one cat to the other. "Who sent you two? In what land can cats speak and catch criminals? And why are these men so strange-looking? They only have two eyes and two hands!" He shudders.

I'm pretty sure the king won't buy my explanation about the other side of the river, so I keep my mouth shut.

"Just give us the staff and we will be on our way," one of the men demands.

"The staff?" the king repeats.

"Didn't you get their note demanding the Staff of Power in exchange for Princess Viola?" Pockets asks, speaking in front of the king for the first time.

"What note?" the king asks.

"This one," Hector says. He reaches into a pocket of fur and pulls out a scroll. He hands the scroll to the king.

"Hector's got pockets in his fur, too!" I whisper to Pockets.

"It's a space cat thing," he whispers back.

"I was able to grab this out of the messenger's bag before it reached the castle," Hector explains. "I couldn't risk your handing over the staff."

The king reads B.U.R.P.'s demands. "I will take it from here," he tells Pockets and Hector. To his knights he says, "Do not let these criminals escape." The knights step forward and place heavy armored hands on the bad guys' shoulders.

Pockets pulls out his phone. "I have to call my father," he explains.

Seems like a strange time to say hi, but when his father answers, Pockets goes into this whole story about how we tried to fit in here, but in the end we had no choice and now the king knows too much. His father's voice booms through the other end of the phone. "You know what you have to do, Pilarbing Fangorious!"

Pockets tries to argue. "Not that! Please, Dad, anyone but—"

His dad hangs up. Pockets grits his teeth, then makes another call. This time I don't hear anything from the other end. But a moment later, a shimmer appears in the air. Before I can blink, a tiny red alien with waving antennae and one big eye stands in front of us. His little round spaceship hovers a few feet above the ground. I gasp in surprise, and I'm not the only one. One of the knights actually *faints*! The king pulls the princess close, but she squirms away to get a closer look.

If Pockets is trying to keep them from knowing about life on other planets, he's not doing a very good job of it by bringing this guy here.

"Hey!" I say to the new arrival. "Where have I seen you before?"

The alien totally ignores me and hurries up to Pockets. He bows deeply. "You called for me, oh noble, glorious one! I always knew this day would come. How can I be of help?"

And I thought Bloppy and that little black cat were fans of Pockets. They've got nothing on this guy! I admit, I'm a little jealous. He's supposed to be MY cool cat!

Pockets grimaces. "Hello, Feemus," he forces himself to say through clenched teeth. "Do what you do best."

The alien salutes Pockets like he's in the army. "Yes, sir!" he says. He turns his one-eyed gaze onto the crowd. Then a beam of red light shoots between his two antennae, and everyone except him, me, the horse, Pockets, and Hector stands

P4

frozen in the middle of whatever they were doing.

Even a bird has stopped in midflight! The princess has one arm out, reaching for Feemus, who steps politely away.

Pockets and Hector spring into action. Pockets slips the staff from the king's hand and replaces it with one almost exactly the same size and shape. "Curtain rod from the haunted castle," he explains with a wink. That cat thinks of everything.

Hector grabs the two bad guys and somehow squeezes them into Feemus's tiny spaceship. He then runs over to the frozen princess and pats her lovingly on the head. "I will miss you, little one," he tells her. "You've got pluck and a natural curiosity. It will serve you well. Once the

Staff of Power is gone from here, you shall be safe again." He pulls out a jousting helmet from one of his pockets and tucks it under Viola's arm. Then he grabs the stuffed bear Pockets had left with him in the shed and sticks it inside the helmet for her to find. With a final bow to the frozen king, he joins his prisoners in Feemus's spaceship.

"I don't understand," I say to Pockets, who is busy untying the horse from the cart. "How did the little red guy freeze everyone? What happens when they unfreeze and we're gone?"

"They won't remember us," Pockets explains. "Feemus has the ability to slow down time until it almost stops. He will replace their memories of the past day and then return them to their normal time frame."

I take one last look around. "Princess Viola won't remember me at all?"

"Sorry, but no," he says.

I hold my hand to my cheek. I will definitely remember her.

Feemus approaches Pockets. "Are you ready, oh amazing one, oh great leader?"

Pockets groans. "Please stop calling me things like that."

"But I am the head of your fan club," Feemus says. "How can I not be thrilled to be in your presence?"

"Fan club?" I repeat in disbelief. "You have a *fan club*?"

"I don't want to talk about it," Pockets says. He turns around and hops up onto the horse's back. He holds out his paw, I grab it, and he hoists me up behind him. I wrap my arms around his belly.

"Wait twenty minutes and then unfreeze them," Pockets instructs Feemus. "That will give us a chance to get back to our landing site and take off. Give the princess the memory that she wandered to the haunted castle and found some stray cats. Perhaps she will go back to feed them and will bring the gardens back to life. It may fulfill her need for adventure a bit."

Feemus bows again. "Yes, Your Wonderfulness. Thank you again for allowing me to be of service. You are truly the bravest, smartest, most—"

I don't hear what other compliments Feemus was about to give, because Pockets turns the horse around and begins to gallop toward the cornfield. I hold on tighter. They should make seat belts on these things!

A memory comes rushing back to me. I lean into Pockets. "Now I remember where I've seen that guy! You wouldn't let him sit with us for lunch at Akbar's a few weeks ago. Why wouldn't you?"

"He's always following me around," Pockets says as we reach the town square. "It was kind of flattering in the beginning, but now it's just embarrassing. He's so... *enthusiastic*." We pass at least twenty people, all frozen in the midst of eating, talking, shopping, or walking. I look for the boys, but they aren't playing their game anymore.

"I think he's sweet," I tell him. "I hope we see him again."

"Trust me, we will."

"Dad!" I shout, scrambling off the horse the second we arrive back at the taxi. I was half-afraid he'd be frozen like everyone else, but he's not. He runs over and scoops me up while Pockets dissolves the camo-spray and makes the taxi reappear.

"Archie! How was it? Did you find the princess before the king gave B.U.R.P. the staff?"

"It turns out he didn't even know they were after it," I explain. "Hector the cat stopped the note before it got to the king, but I found the princess and she thought she was going to see a circus! And did you know Pockets has a fan club?"

"Hector the cat?" he asks. "A circus? A fan club? Sounds like you've got a long story to tell me."

"It will have to wait for the ride home," Pockets says. "We need to leave right now." He jumps into the backseat of the taxi and settles in for his usual post-adventure nap.

"Ahem," Dad says, clearing his throat. "Forget something?" He waves his third arm in the air.

"Oops," Pockets says. He pulls out the Atom Assembler and zaps us both. It tingles just as much as last time. I'm going to miss my three eyes. It was kinda cool being able to see in the dark without those goggles.

"Hey, Dad," I ask as we climb in the

front seat, "did you know we only had two toes on this planet?"

He is busy admiring his full head of hair in the rearview mirror and doesn't hear me. It will just have to be my little secret.

CHAPTER EiGHT:
Happily Ever After

Once we are safely out of sight of Tri-Dark, we can finally relax. Pockets sends a message to his dad. He reports that the cat-loving boy in the black cloak is an important member of B.U.R.P. and that he is still on the loose. He makes sure to mention my role in helping on the mission, which is very nice of him. Then he puts away his screen and pulls out his pillow.

Dad calls headquarters to check in. Minerva is finally back, but she is not happy.

"Morningstar!" she shouts. "I just got a call from the taxi depot on Libra 6. They said your pickup—one Mr. Bloppy—never arrived yesterday. Explain?"

"Didn't you get my messages?" Dad asks. "We had to drop Bloppy at Akbar's. I told you that we had an important mission and that I needed another driver to take him the rest of the way."

"I received no such message," Minerva says.

Dad and I exchange a worried look. "So he's still at Akbar's?" Dad asks.

"I have no idea," Minerva says.

"We're on our way," Dad says.

"I blame that cat," Minerva grumbles.

Dad switches off the com. I map out the fastest way to get there.

When we arrive, Dad, Pockets, and I run all over Akbar's calling Bloppy's name. We keep asking, but no one has seen him, which is strange because he's not someone you could easily miss. Plus, he's wearing a name tag. Pockets ducks into Barney's to grab us all some bagels (of course) while Dad and I keep looking. We wind up back where we started, in the gift shop. A sign on the wall catches my eye. It's different from the one we saw last time.

WHETHER YOU'VE GOT YOUR
OWN WHEELS OR NEED
TO BORROW OURS,
VISIT AKBAR'S ROLLER RINK!
WE NOW HAVE THE SHINIEST,
SMOOTHEST FLOORS THIS SIDE
OF THE VIRGO SUPERCLUSTER.
SO ROLL ON IN AND TAKE
A SPIN!

The shiniest, smoothest floors! I know someone who can make a floor supershiny!

Sure enough, we spot Bloppy as soon as we reach the roller rink. He's standing in the center of the rink, dripping goop everywhere. Creatures with all number of legs skate happily around him. He breaks into a huge grin when he sees us. He looks much happier than when we picked him up on Earth.

"Sal and Archie Morningstar!" he cries out. "How lovely to see you!"

We run onto the rink, slipping and sliding as we go. "We are so glad to see you, too," Dad says. "I'm sorry! There was a mix-up and no taxi was sent to get you yesterday. But I can drive you now."

Bloppy's smile doesn't fade. "Your dropping me here was the best thing that could have happened. This is the perfect job for me. Everyone at Akbar's is so nice." He leans close to us and lowers his voice. "And I met a special someone." He tilts his head toward the other side of the rink.

At first I think I'm seeing Bloppy in the mirror, but *this* Bloppy is pink instead of orange and is wearing a pink bow on her head. I can't read her name tag from this far away, but I can see she's wearing one.

Dad grins and slaps Bloppy on the shoulder. "Way to go, dude. She's a keeper."

"I know," Bloppy says, waving to the girl. She waves back with both arms. As she does, huge, gooey pink globs fall from her hands and splat across the floor. The skaters around her cheer.

We promise Bloppy we will visit whenever we're in the neighborhood. He hugs us both good-bye. I don't know what Pockets was making such a big fuss about. It's a nice, cozy, only mildly oozy hug.

It's dark again by the time we finally arrive home to our apartment on Earth.

Mom gives me a huge hug and says I look older, which I'm sure I don't, even if I did rescue a princess.

Penny's light is still on, so I go in to say good night. She looks up at me with big, sleepy eyes. "Story?" she asks.

Even though I'm *sooooo* tired, I sit down on the edge of her bed and begin. "Once upon a time, there was a beautiful princess named Viola who liked to joust. And when she ate beans, well, she could burp louder than anybody!"

Penny giggles.

"One day she met a group of circus performers and..."

Penny snores. She and Pockets and Dad have a lot in common—they all fall asleep quickly and make a lot of noise

when they sleep. The rest of the story will have to wait till tomorrow night. Unless I'm off on another adventure! For now, though, I'm happy to be back home. As I get up to leave, Pockets comes in, jumps onto the bed, turns in circles a few times, and then curls up and begins licking his paws.

"Hey, Pockets," I whisper. "Is that Feemus outside Penny's window?"

"Aaaaahhh!" He scrambles off the bed and zips underneath it.

I'll tell him I was only kidding in the morning.

Three Science Facts to Impress Your Friends and Teachers

1. LIGHT plays an important role in Archie's adventure to planet Tri-Dark, where electricity hasn't been invented yet. Light is made up of particles called **PHOTONS**, and they travel in waves, like the kind you'd see in the ocean. Each color of visible light has a different wavelength—purple has the shortest, and red has the longest. Light will bounce off a mirror or bend in water.

114

2. Archie is not able to see many stars at home on Earth because of all the outside lights in the city at night. The light shines up into the sky, and then our atmosphere scatters it and sends it back down at us, blocking our view of the stars. Since there is no electric light on Tri-Dark, Archie is able to see all the stars clearly, as our ancestors would have been able to on Earth. LiGH† POLLU†iON not only blocks our ability to see into space, but it causes migrating birds to go off course, and it confuses nocturnal animals that come out at night and need the darkness. Light pollution also wastes energy by sending light into the sky, where it is not needed.

3. Archie's dad uses **NiGH† ViSiON GOGGLES** so he can see in the dark to land his space taxi on Tri-Dark. There are two types of night vision goggles. The first type is called **iMaGE ENHaNCEMEN†**, which is the type Archie, his dad, and Pockets use in the story. The goggles collect any available light reflected off an object (even infrared, which the human eye normally can't see). The light is then passed through a series of lenses, allowing the person wearing the goggles to see in the dark. The other type of night vision goggles is called **†HERMaL iMaGiNG.** This type detects light that is emitted by objects in the form of heat, and allows the wearer to see the images based on how warm something is. This would be helpful if Archie was trying to find Pockets in the dark.

WENDY MASS has written lots of books for kids. MICHAEL BRAWER is a teacher who drives space taxis on the side. They live in New Jersey with their two kids and two cats, none of whom have left the solar system.